Tell Me a Story, Please

Kyoko Hara
Kazue Takahashi

Museyon
New York

"Mama, tell me a story, please," Yuka said and handed a book of fairy tales to her mother.

"Can't you read that on your own, Yuka?" Mama asked and put down her knitting.

"I can, but I want you to read it for me, Mama."

Yuka was a first grader, and she could read on her own. But ever since she was a baby, Yuka had loved her mother reading to her because Mama was very good at imitating the voices

of all the different characters
in the stories.

"Alright, alright. Where should
we start?"

Yuka snuggled next to her mother
and opened to a page in the book.

"Here's good, Mama."

"Okay! Long ago there was a girl
called Little Red Riding Hood."

The story was a little scary for Yuka, but she loved it anyway.

"One day, when Little Red Riding Hood was on her way to visit her sick grandmother she met a bad wolf."

Mama used a wheedling tone when the wolf was trying to get friendly with Little Red Riding Hood, and did the fake voice he used when he pretended to be her grandmother.

Sometimes she would even do a wailing voice for the wolf, though it wasn't written in Yuka's book.

". . . And then together with her grandmother, Little Red Riding Hood happily ate the cake that she had brought. The end."

Mama closed the book and handed it back to Yuka.

"That was fun! Let's read one more."

Yuka opened the book again, but Mama turned to her and said, "Yuka, the baby is going to be born soon. Will you be nice to your new little brother or sister?"

"I will, Mama. I'm really looking forward to being a big sister!" Yuka said as she laid her cheek on Mama's stomach.

Yuka had a brother named Kenta, who was three years older than her. But he was always playing soccer and never played with Yuka. And if they ever got cake for a snack, he'd always take the largest piece. A few days earlier when Mama wasn't looking, he stole fried chicken from Yuka's plate.

When she complained, instead of apologizing, Kenta said, "I can do it, because I'm three years older," then he pulled her hair.

Whether she got a little sister or little brother, Yuka swore she would be much nicer and play with the baby a lot more.

The day after Mama left for the hospital with her big belly, Yuka went with Papa and Kenta to visit her. Next to Mama slept an itty-bitty baby. Yuka stared down at it and gently touched the baby's cheek. It was warm, soft, and smelled nice.

"Yuka and Kenta, this is your little brother, Yuto. Please love him."

"I will! I promise!"

Yuka grinned and wrapped her pinky around Mama's.

When Mama came home from the hospital with Yuto, Yuka's life changed a little. Up till now, when Yuka would return from school she and Mama would talk about their days while enjoying some snacks. But now, Mama would feed Yuto his milk, and change his diapers, and always looked busy.

Any time Yuka said, "Hey, Mama," Mama would answer, "Just a minute," as if she wasn't really listening.

What Yuka was especially
disappointed about was that
Mama no longer read to her.
One day, when Yuka had tried
to bring a book to her while
Yuto was taking a nap, Mama
said, "I'm sorry, I have to do the
laundry now. Why don't you ask
your brother?"

"You said the same thing last
time," Yuka said.

Yuka felt very lonely. She thought
it might have been better if her little
brother had never come home.

Yuka peeked into Kenta's room.
"Kenta, can you read to me?" she
asked. But he was about to head out.

"I'm going to practice soccer now.
I don't have time for that stuff."

"Hmph!" Yuka huffed.

But then, through the window,
Yuka saw the old lady next door
tending to the flowers in her garden.

I know!

Yuka took her book and walked over to the next-door neighbor.

"Hello, ma'am!"

"Why hello, Yuka."

"Um, I was wondering if you could read me a story."

"Why of course. Come in."

The two sat on the couch inside and opened the book.

"Alright, let's see here. Once upon a time . . . "

Five lines into the story the old lady's voice suddenly stopped.

Yuka looked over and saw the old lady had started to nod off. Yuka sighed and gently took the book off the old lady's lap, then quietly made her way out of the house.

"Aww, isn't there anyone who will read to me?"

"Hi, Yuka! What are you up to?"

Someone tapped Yuka's shoulder. When she turned around, she saw the young lady who lived across the street.

"Hello! Oh, um, actually if you—" Yuka began to say.

"Oh, I'm sorry. I'm late for my date! I'll see you around!"

She gave Yuka a big wave goodbye and hurried away down the street.

"Goodbye," Yuka responded with a small wave, and trudged away with her book in hand.

She walked for a while and then came across an empty lot. At one point a mansion had stood there, but now many new trees and grass had grown in the large lot and it had become its own little forest with a maple tree at its center. Yuka sometimes came here to pick flowers and to gather acorns and leaves.

She sat down underneath the maple tree. All she could hear was the gentle rustling of the fall-colored leaves in the breeze.

"Ahh-ahh, I'm so bored," Yuka said to herself, and her voice resounded through the forest.

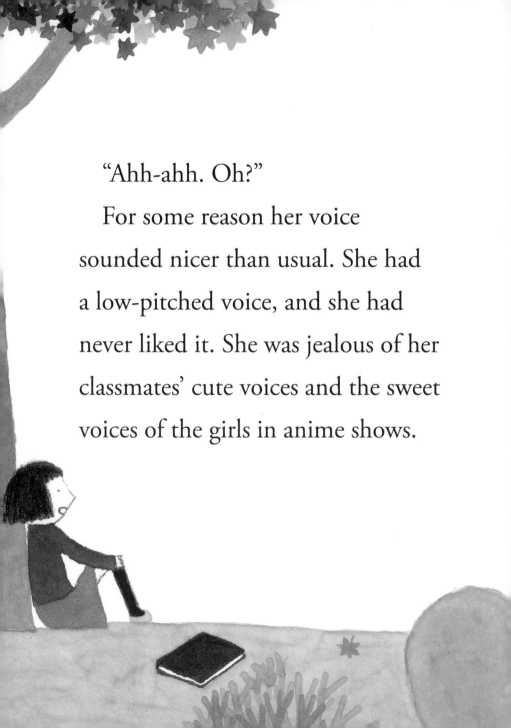

"Ahh-ahh. Oh?"

For some reason her voice sounded nicer than usual. She had a low-pitched voice, and she had never liked it. She was jealous of her classmates' cute voices and the sweet voices of the girls in anime shows.

That was why she always hated having to read in front of the class at school. Just standing up made her heart race. She'd stumble over her words, and the more the teacher focused on her, the lower and quieter her voice would get. But now there wasn't anyone around. Yuka opened her book and began to read aloud.

"The story of *Snow White*. Once upon a time, there lived a king and his queen.

"The queen gave birth to a beautiful baby girl with skin as white as snow. They named her Snow White."

Yuka felt good reading the words on the page. It seemed that her voice sounded clearer and better here.

"One day, Snow White was—"

Rustle, rustle, crunch, rustle. Yuka heard faint sounds. She looked up into the tree.

A squirrel was
watching from the
end of a branch.
Yuka's eyes opened
wide. She thought she
shouldn't scare it,
so slowly she turned her face back
to the book and began to read.
After a bit, came another
rustle, rustle, crunch, rustle.
Yuka looked up and saw a rabbit in
front of her. It looked straight at her.
"Oh. . . ."

While Yuka gaped, the rabbit spoke, "Please, read more."

Yuka was completely shocked but nodded and continued to the end.

". . . And Snow White lived happily ever after."

Yuka lifted her eyes from the book. Without her knowing it, a fox, a raccoon, a dog, a monkey, a bear, and a variety of other animals had gathered around her.

"That was a very fun story!"

"You have a lovely voice!" the animals said, and they gave her a round of applause.

Then, at the same time, the animals all said, "Read us another story."

"Okay, sure!" Yuka was very pleased. This time she read *Momotaro: The Peach Boy*, a Japanese folktale about a boy named Momotaro who was born from a peach. Along with

his animal companions, he fights and conquers the bad guys on Ogre Island.

The dog, the monkey, and the pheasant glowed with pride at the scene where those same animals join Momotaro's journey to Ogre Island. The other animals looked on with envy at the three.

When Yuka got to the part where they defeat the ogre, the animals cheered.

Before Yuka knew it, the breeze had gotten a bit chillier.

"I have to go home. Mama is probably worried," she said.

When Yuka stood up with the book in her hands, all the animals looked disappointed.

"What's your name?"

"Will you be back?"

"Will you come and read to us again?"

Yuka grinned broadly and nodded.

"My name is Yuka. I'll come again next Saturday. I'll see you then. Goodbye."

"We'll be waiting. Goodbye!"

The animals all waved to her.

"I'm home!" Yuka said as she opened the front door. She was met by Mama holding her sleeping baby brother.

"Welcome home, Yuka. Would you like a snack?"

"Yes!"

Yuka washed her hands and enjoyed a glass of milk and a chocolate cookie.

"You look very happy. Did you find somewhere fun to play today?" Mama asked her.

"Yup! I read some stories to . . . my friends today."

"Oh, I see," Mama said happily. "Will you read to me too, Yuka."

"Sure, I will next time," Yuka giggled.

When Yuka went back to her own room, she opened her book of fairy tales and happily whispered to herself, "Which story should I read to everyone next time?"

The next day was Sunday. Yuka
and Mama went shopping while Papa
looked after Yuto. On the way, Yuka
noticed a few men in the forest she
had been in yesterday.

Not many people go over there.
I wonder what they're doing, Yuka
thought, tilting her head.

The fall leaves were even more
golden and crisp the following
Saturday. Yuka took her book of
fairy tales and went to the maple tree
in the forest. She sat at the base of
the tree, and before she knew it, the
animals began to gather around her.

"Hello, Yuka!"

"Tell us a story, please!"

"Okay. Where to begin? Ah yes,
let's read this one."

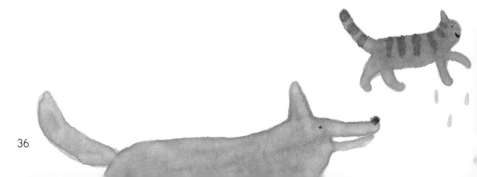

Yuka opened the fairy tale book
and began to read *The Three Little
Pigs*. The story is about three pigs who
combine their efforts to outwit an
evil wolf.

After Yuka finished reading, the
wolf looked upset.

"I'm not mean and a bully like that one," he said.

"That's right. You're very kind, Mr. Wolf," the bear replied.

"For sure! It's just the wolf in this story who is a bully," Yuka added very quickly.

"Let's move on to the next story," Yuka said as she flipped through the pages of the book. She stopped at *Urashima Taro*: *The Fisherman Lad* and began to read.

It is a Japanese folktale about a young fisherman named Urashima Taro, who rescues a turtle. In return, the turtle takes Taro to the palace of the Dragon King.

In the palace, Princess Otohime entertains Taro for a couple of days. But when Taro returns home he finds that hundreds of years have passed. At the end of the story he opens a jewelry box that Otohime had gifted him and forbidden him to open and he turns into an old man.

"The end," Yuka said and looked up.

"That was an interesting story. But it only has a turtle and fish in it. Hey, are there any stories in which I appear?" the raccoon asked.

"That's right. The story before had a dog, a monkey, and a pheasant in it.

I want to hear a story that has me in it too," the fox chimed in.

"My story was about how I bully the little pigs. I'd like a story about a nice wolf," the wolf called out.

The other animals also begged Yuka, saying, "Me too! Me, me! Can I have one too?"

"Okay, okay. I have to head home now, but I'll look for a story that everyone's in for next time."

"Really? Yay!"

"I'm so happy!"

"We'll be waiting for when you come back!"

The animals lined up underneath
the tree and waved goodbye to Yuka
as she headed home.

At home, Yuka read through the
fairy tale book again, but couldn't find
a story in which all the animals in the
forest appeared.

"Oh no. I promised them. What
am I going to do now?" Yuka sighed.

The next day and the day after that,
Yuka went through book after book.
Finally she found a picture book
called *The Bremen Town Musicians*.

In the story, a donkey, a dog, a cat,
and a rooster travel to the town of
Bremen to become musicians.

On their journey they come across
a vacant house where they rest for
the night.

While there, they discover some
robbers who are up to no good,
and together they make threatening
sounds that drive the robbers away.

Yuka's face suddenly
lit up.

"That's it! I have a
great idea. If I swap
the donkey and
rooster in the story
for the animals in
the forest, it will be
perfect!"

Yuka felt happy
when she thought
of the animals in
the forest, and she
adapted the story so
it included them all.
Then she wrote the
new version in her
notebook.

On Wednesday, when Yuka was returning home from her piano lesson, she saw, once again, a group of adults standing around the maple tree in the lot.

"Where are the animals hiding? I hope they don't find my friends."

Yuka felt worried.

After finishing lunch that Saturday, Yuka took the notebook in which she had written the story and headed for the maple tree in the forest.

She sat under the tree with its red and yellow leaves, and all the animals began to gather.

"Yuka! We've waited for you."

"Tell us a story, please!"

"I will, but today I'd like everyone's help in telling the story."

"Really?"

"Will it be difficult?"

"What do we need to do?"

"Are you sure we can do it?" the animals asked, exchanging glances.

"You'll all be fine. I'll let you know when I need your help."

Yuka smiled brightly. She opened her notebook and began reading.

Once upon a time, there was a lonely dog who got old and could no longer work. However, he had a very good voice so he decided to travel to Bremen to join a band.

On his way, he met a bear,

a boar, a wolf, a fox, a raccoon,
a rabbit, a cat, a squirrel,
a pheasant, and a monkey.

They joined together and traveled to Bremen. When night came, the group found a vacant house and decided to rest there until morning.

The forest animals all listened excitedly as they heard themselves appear in the story.

As everyone went to bed, the door of the house opened, and three men stepped inside. The trio lit a candle in the room next to the animals and began to eat and drink and talk.

The animals listened, and realized the three were making plans for a robbery!

The animals shared their ideas, discussed what to do, and then began to move very quietly.

First, the boar climbed onto the bear's back, then the wolf on top of the boar, then the dog, the raccoon, the fox, the monkey, the cat, the rabbit, the pheasant, and the squirrel.

"Now, everyone, try climbing on each other by size," Yuka instructed.

The animals
climbed on top
of each other, just
like in the story,
with the bear at
the bottom.

Yuka continued to read.

The bear whispered to
the others, "Alright,
everyone together!"
Then . . .
"QUAA, CLUCK, THUMP,
MEOW, OOO EEE, BARK,
CHITTER, WOOF, AWOOO,
OINK, GROWL!"
They yelled together and
charged into the dark room
next door.

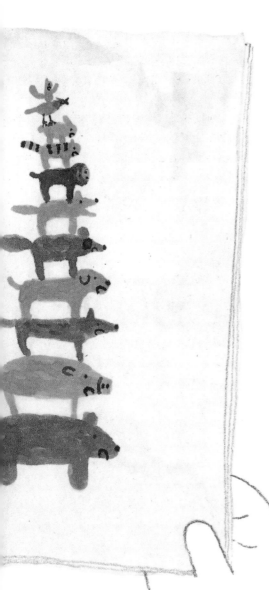

Yuka read up
until that point and
then said, "Ready,
everyone? One,
two, three,

NOW! "

And just like in
the story, the forest
animals all hollered.

QUAA QUAA!

CLUCK CLUCK!

THUMP THUMP!

MEOOOOOW!

OOO EEE!

BAAARK!

CHITTERRR!

AWOOOOOOOOOO!

WOOOF!

OIINK
OIIINK!

"R-run! It's a monster!"

"Forgive us! We won't do anything bad again!" the robbers screamed, stumbling and scrambling out the door. They ran away and never came back.

The animals *all* became good friends and no longer felt lonely. They continued to live in the house, singing and having fun every day.

The End

GROOOOOWL!

When Yuka closed her notebook, all
the forest animals broke out into loud
and happy applause.

"That was such fun, Yuka!"

"If we join together, like in the story—"

"There's nothing
we can't do!"
"That's right!"
The forest animals
exchanged glances.

At that moment, a sudden gust of cold wind blew, and Yuka sneezed twice.

Autumn would soon be over, and the trees would lose all their leaves.

"It will be winter shortly," the raccoon said.

"Yeah. Squirrel and I will sleep through the cold winter, and no one else will be outside much. So, we won't be able to see you, Yuka," the bear said.

"That's so sad. Will I see you again in the spring?" Yuka asked.

"Of course. I'm sure we'll meet again. We want to hear more of Yuka's stories," said the rabbit.

"Yeah! We'll try our best to make it until then," said the monkey, raising his fist in the air.

"What's the matter? It's too bad that I can't see you for a while, but you'll just stay home through winter, right?" Yuka let out a little giggle.

"Hehe, I guess you're right," the monkey said, scratching his head.

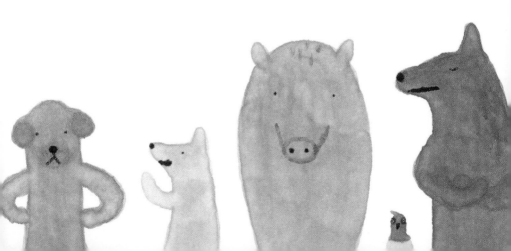

"Alright, everyone! I'll see you soon!"

"Thank you for all the fun stories, Yuka!"

The animals waved, then they discussed something amongst themselves and nodded.

At home, Yuka didn't feel well. She had caught a cold and had a fever. It was hard for her to stay in bed for several days and take her medicine. But her grandmother came and took care of Yuto, so for the first time in a while Mama was able to be by Yuka's side and read her a story.

"Thank you, Mama. When I get better, I'll read for you. You know, the other day in class, my teacher said my reading had improved."

"Wow! That's wonderful. You've been doing such a great job," Mama said happily, as she stroked Yuka's hair.

On the day Yuka finally got over her cold, snow was falling lightly from the sky.

I wonder if everyone in the forest is sleeping, Yuka thought as she looked out the window.

Later that night while they were eating dinner, Papa said, "Wasn't there talk of building a new apartment complex where the forest with the big maple tree is?"

"What! Really?" Yuka dropped her chopsticks in surprise. It was the first time she had heard this.

"Yes, but it seems like they gave up on the project."

"Well, that's good! Everyone in the neighborhood was against them cutting down such a magnificent tree," Mama added.

"Sure, there were definitely a lot of people who opposed it but . . . " Papa looked puzzled.

"What?" Yuka and Mama asked at the same time.

"Whenever people went to the forest to inspect the construction work, they saw the shadow of a gigantic animal and heard ominous sounds. The landowner said that nature itself was telling them to not cut down such a beautiful tree. Now he has cancelled the project."

"Nah! I don't believe it," Kenta said loudly.

But Yuka knew immediately what had happened. The animals in the forest must have combined their power, just like in *The Bremen Town Musicians*.

"That's great! So, then they'll leave that tree and forest alone, Papa?"

"They will. You also love that forest, don't you, Yuka? We must preserve such a splendid tree, right?" Papa nodded and smiled.

Yuka was so happy. As soon as she went into her room, she brought out her notebook and read aloud her altered version of *The Bremen Town Musicians*.

Yuka knew that all her forest friends were safe now and sleeping soundly.

*When spring comes and it is warm
I will go see everyone in the forest again
with my book,* Yuka thought. *And this
time I'll bring my little brother Yuto and
I'll read to him too!*